WHERE'S WALLY?
AT SEA
MARTIN HANDFORD

WALKER BOOKS
AND SUBSIDIARIES
LONDON • BOSTON • SYDNEY • AUCKLAND

AHOY, WALLY FANS!

COME WITH ME ON A WET AND WILD ADVENTURE! WE'LL "SEA" (HA, HA!) MANY PEOPLE ON THE BEACH AND IN THE WATER, AS WELL AS PESKY PIRATES AND VILLAINOUS VIKINGS ON THE HUNT FOR TREASURE. WATCH OUT FOR CRAZY UNDERWATER CREATURES TOO! INCREDIBLE!

TO:

WALLY MATES,

DOWN THE PLUGHOLE,

UP THE CREEK.

THERE ARE LOTS OF FIN-TASTIC GAMES AND PUZZLES FOR US TO PLAY ON OUR JOURNEY AND THEY'RE ALL COMPLETELY BARNACLES!

CAN YOU ALSO HELP FIND THIS PRECIOUS SHELL?

AND I ALMOST FORGOT, LIKE A SAILING KNOT... MY FRIENDS, WOOF, WENDA, WIZARD WHITEBEARD AND

ODLAW ARE HEADING OUT TO SEA WITH US. KEEP YOUR BINOCULARS CLOSE BY IN CASE YOU SPOT ANY OF OUR LOST THINGS.

WALLY'S KEY   WOOF'S BONE   WENDA'S CAMERA   WIZARD WHITEBEARD'S SCROLL   ODLAW'S BINOCULARS

ANCHORS AWEIGH! DIVE ON IN!

Wally

SEA SILHOUETTES

Study this busy beach scene to
find each silhouette. Phew,
what a sizzling search!

GONE FISHING

Which fisherman caught a jellyfish? Also find one fish within each shoal of yellow, pink, blue and green fish with different coloured fins.

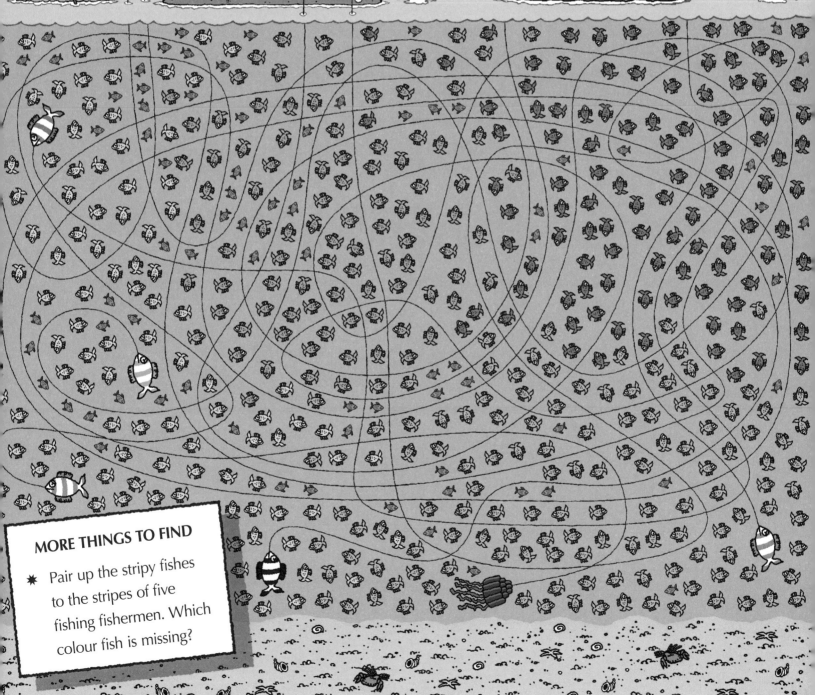

MORE THINGS TO FIND

★ Pair up the stripy fishes to the stripes of five fishing fishermen. Which colour fish is missing?

BOAT-RACE-DAY

Wow! What a wacky boat bonanza! There are six different races all happening at once. Can you match up the sets of flags to find out which boats are entered into which competition? There's my rowing boat race; Woof's speedboat race; Wenda's build-your-own-raft race; Wizard Whitebeard's sailing race; Odlaw's treasure hunt and a who-can-catch-the-most-fish race.

Clue: First, search for me and my friends to find out which race is which!

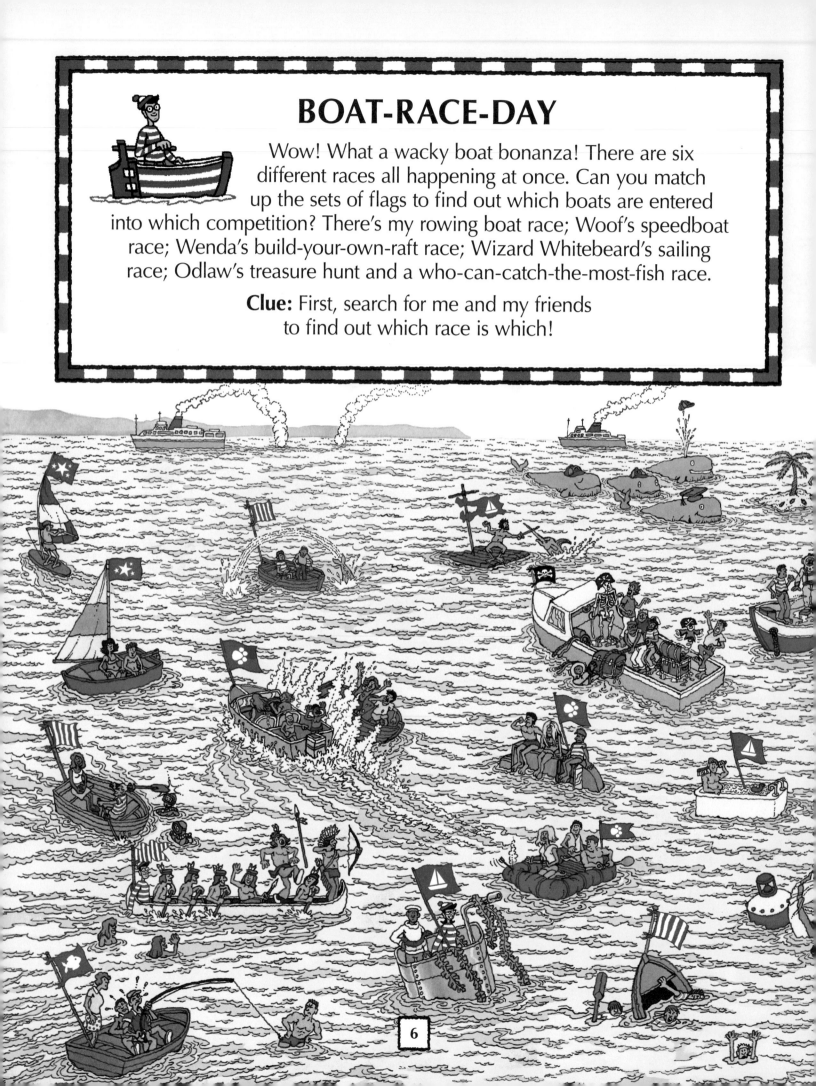

SECRET SWIMATHON

Follow my wanders across the open waters until you find
the one boat with treasure stashed on-board.

❶ **First**, find a boat with a trail of steam that rises in and out of the water.
❷ **Jump overboard** and swim to a "school". Have a whale of a time!
❸ **Carry on past** a swordfight, to a wise Indian wearing a three-feathered
headdress. ❹ **"Duck" underwater** to one thing that is rubber and red
but not inflatable. ❺ **Swim behind** a "sea bed" to mermaids. Avoid
the tangled water-skiers! ❻ **Spy** a bull and he will help you aboard!

THE TREASURE TRAMPLE

First find me, and from there draw a straight line passing through all five of my co-ordinates. Then do the same for Odlaw and Wenda. Can you find the square where we all cross paths? Pirate treasure is buried here!

MORE THINGS TO DO

* Make your own treasure hunt! Hide a *Where's Wally?* book in your house and leave clues for friends or family to find it!

CO-ORDINATES

WALLY: D1; D4; C4; C5; E5

ODLAW: A5; B5; B2; D2; D3

WENDA: B3; C3; C2; E2; E1

NORSE CODE

Decode the second message to help you find a treasure map on this page. Start by copying over any letters with the same Norse letter, then fill in the blanks.

MESSAGE ONE

ᛉ	ᛒ	ᚲ	ᛒ	ᛖ	ᛏ	ᚷ	ᛊ	ᛝ	ᚱ	ᛁ	ᛗ	ᛝ
V	I	K	I	N	G	S		A	R	E		

ᛜ	ᛝ	ᚾ	ᛚ	ᚠ	ᛠ	ᛊ	ᛝ	ᛏ	ᛁ	ᛒ	ᛗ	ᛠ	ᛊ
O	D	L	A	W	S		F	R	I	E	N	D	S

MESSAGE TWO

ᛗ	ᚠ	ᚲ	ᛝ	ᛒ	ᛖ	ᛝ	ᚾ	ᚠ	ᛏ	ᛠ	ᛝ

ᛏ	ᛜ	ᛁ	ᛝ	ᚲ	ᛒ	ᛒ	ᛁ	ᚠ	ᛏ	ᛗ	ᛝ	ᚷ	ᛜ	ᚾ	ᛝ

SNAKY SEARCH

Find the "S" words in the wordsearch below. Letters must run continuously but they can go in any direction as long as the sides of their squares touch. Sssneaky!

Stripes
Slippery
Sea snake
Scaly skin
Spots
Snakebite

MORE THINGS TO FIND

* One repeated word that is backwards.

* A word that isn't a snake (but you might mistake it for one!).

FISH FOOD

Look behind you! Who is going to eat who? Put these comic strip pictures in order by numbering the white shells from 1–7.

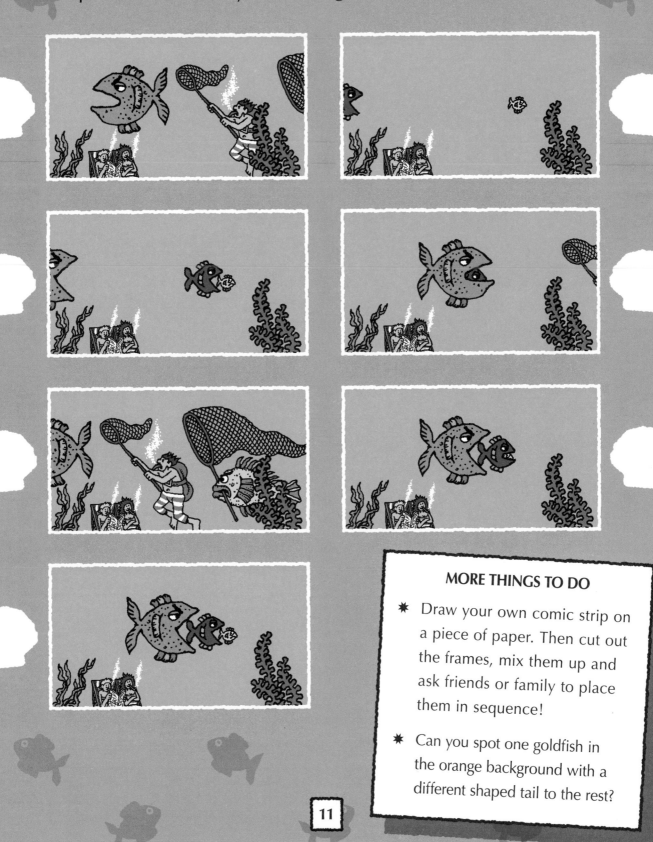

MORE THINGS TO DO

* Draw your own comic strip on a piece of paper. Then cut out the frames, mix them up and ask friends or family to place them in sequence!

* Can you spot one goldfish in the orange background with a different shaped tail to the rest?

PIECES OF EIGHT

Look closely at the pictures in the coins to find out which ones are in the scene. Be warned, four of them are from elsewhere in the book! Yo, ho, ho!

MORE THINGS TO DO

* Being a pirate is all about luck! Toss a coin eight times – heads, you're a pirate, tails you're a fisherman!

SEASHELLS GALORE

I see seashells on the seashore! Seek out and colour in only the shells,
not the pebbles, to reveal four items washed ashore.

MORE THINGS TO DO

✱ When you're next at
the beach with a friend,
collect flat stones (the size
of a 1p coin). Take it in
turns to stack them. The
winner is the one who
doesn't topple the tower.

SEA SETS

Match each sea creature, scuba-diver and item under the sea with one or more identical copies to find an odd one out. It's maritime mayhem down there!

MORE THINGS TO DO

✷ What do you call a fish without an eye? "Fsh"

✷ How do you make an octopus laugh? With ten-tickles

PIRATEY PUZZLE

Avast, me hearties! What a puzzling picture! Can you find the correct three missing pieces? Arrr!

MESSAGE IN A BOTTLE

Can you find eight real words by matching up the pairs of papers?
Write your answers in the bottle below. You can use each piece
more than once and four ripped edges pair together perfectly.

LOLLY

SAND

SHIP

HORSE

CREAM

PIRATE

CASTLE

SHELL

SEA

QUICK

ICE

WRECK

1.....................
2.....................
3.....................
4.....................
5.....................
6.....................
7.....................
8.....................

MAKE A MONSTROSITY

Create your very own sea creature and colour in the surrounding scene. What do you think is lurking at the bottom of this deep, dark sea? Eeek!

18

FISHING NET SETS

What a catch! Draw in the missing treasure trinkets. All nine must appear once in each box, but never in the same row.

DEEP SEA DIVE

Choose a start picture. Then move to any square that shares one identical creature (including colour). The squares do not have to be touching. Keep going until you find a combination that gets you to a finish. Your moves will take you all over the place! You can go diagonally, down and up and down again and jump however many rows you like.

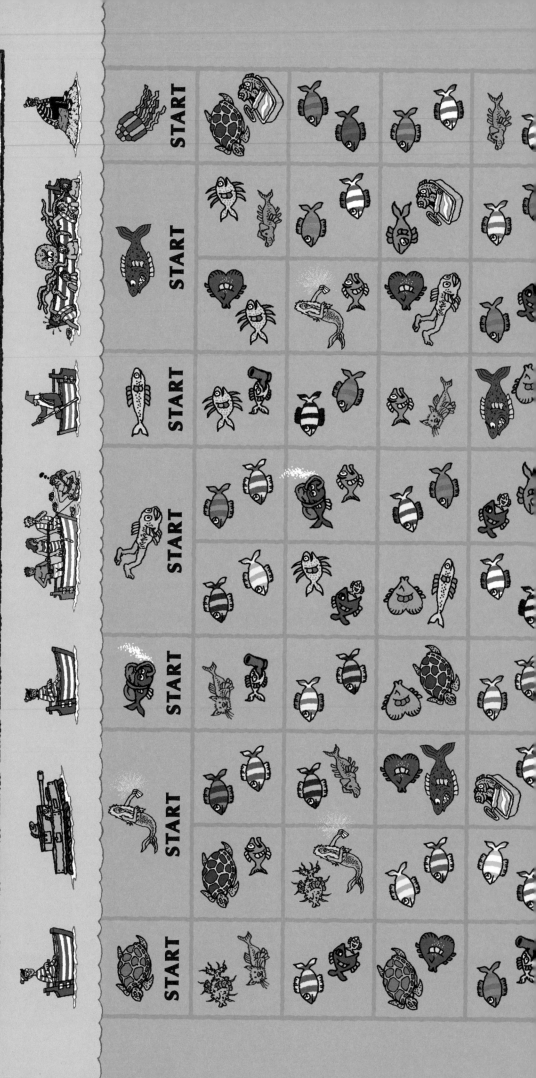

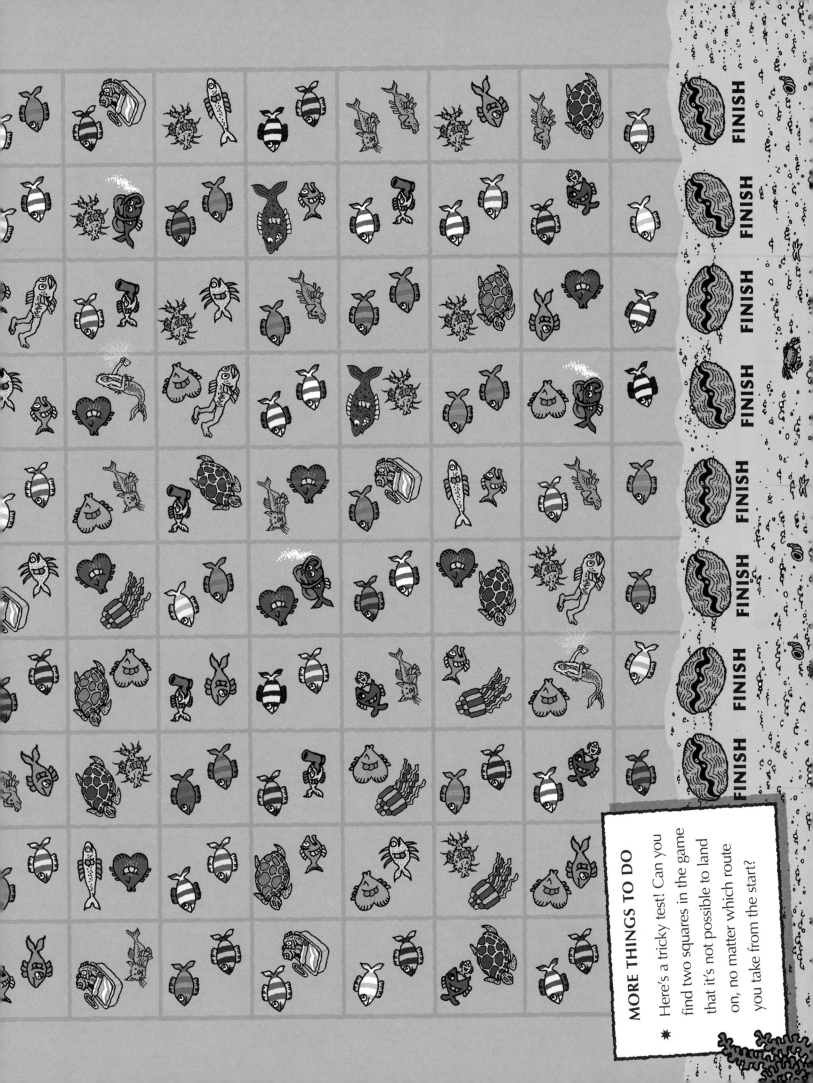

FINISH FINISH FINISH FINISH FINISH FINISH FINISH FINISH

MORE THINGS TO DO

* Here's a tricky test! Can you find two squares in the game that it's not possible to land on, no matter which route you take from the start?

BLOWING BUBBLES

Glug, glug! Strike through the three letters that spell
the word "pop" in each bubble, then unscramble
the rest of the letters to spell eleven words.

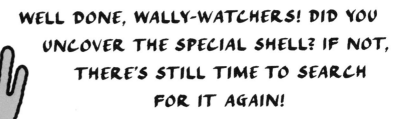

WELL DONE, WALLY-WATCHERS! DID YOU UNCOVER THE SPECIAL SHELL? IF NOT, THERE'S STILL TIME TO SEARCH FOR IT AGAIN!

WAIT, THERE'S MORE! LOOK BACK THROUGH THE PICTURES TO FIND THE ITEMS ON THE CHECKLIST AND SHOWN IN THE STRIPY SHAPES BELOW.

HAVE EEL-Y GOOD FUN!

Wally

AT SEA CHECKLIST

- [ ] Eighteen orange crabs
- [ ] A punctured lilo
- [ ] Two men falling out of a palm tree
- [ ] A fishbowl
- [ ] Two "fish tanks"
- [ ] A cowboy riding a sea horse
- [ ] Ten electric eels
- [ ] A whale disguised as a rock
- [ ] Two shark-surrounded rocks
- [ ] Five sea "lions"
- [ ] A fish with five boat-shaped silhouettes on its side
- [ ] Three green octopuses
- [ ] Two men hooked by fishing lines
- [ ] A red-and-yellow umbrella
- [ ] Fish jumping through a boat's sail
- [ ] A man-shaped hole in a pirate ship sail
- [ ] Seven "saw" fish
- [ ] Three pirates with hooks for hands
- [ ] Three beach balls
- [ ] Three fish wearing bobble hats
- [ ] Wally, Woof, Wenda, Wizard Whitebeard and Odlaw hiding behind seaweed

HERE ARE SOME ANSWERS TO THE HARDEST PUZZLES. DON'T GIVE UP ON THE OTHERS – WHY NOT ASK YOUR FRIENDS TO HELP?

GONE FISHING

A red stripy fish is missing.

BOAT-RACE-DAY

 Wally's rowing boat race

 Woof's speedboat race

 Wenda's build-your-own-raft race

Wizard Whitebeard's sailing race

Odlaw's treasure hunt

The who-can-catch-the-most-fish race

THE TREASURE TRAMPLE

D2

NORSE CODE

MAP IN HAND FOR PIRATE GOLD

First published 2016 by Walker Books Ltd, 87 Vauxhall Walk, London SE11 5HJ • 2 4 6 8 10 9 7 5 3 1 • © 1987–2016 Martin Handford • The right of Martin Handford to be identified as author/illustrator of this work has been asserted by him in accordance with the Copyright, Designs and Patents Act 1988. • This book has been typeset in Wallyfont and Optima • Printed in China • All rights reserved. • British Library Cataloguing in Publication Data: a catalogue record for this book is available from the British Library. • ISBN 978-1-4063-7061-4 • www.walker.co.uk

SNAKY SEARCH

MESSAGE IN A BOTTLE

Sandcastle; Quicksand. Ice lolly; Ice cream. Pirate ship; Shipwreck. Seahorse; Seashell

FISHING NET SETS

BLOWING BUBBLES

Mermaid; Seaweed; Turtle; Snorkel; Squid; Yacht; Island; Shark; Reef; Crab; Tide

ONE LAST THING

Did you spot a fish that Wizard Whitebeard made with his magic? It's red, white and blue and has stars on it too. Wow!